My Bodyguard

JOE CLARO

SCHOLASTIC BOOK SERVICES
New York Toronto London Auckland Sydney Tokyo

MELVIN SIMON PRODUCTIONS PRESENTS
A TONY BILL FILM
MY BODYGUARD
starring
CHRIS MAKEPEACE
RUTH GORDON
MATT DILLON

Based on the screenplay by
ALAN ORMSBY

ISBN 0-590-31932-9

12 11 10 9 8 7 6 5 4 3 2 1   11   0 1 2 3 4 5/8

CHAPTER 1

The sun was just about gone for the day, and the breeze coming off Lake Michigan was cooling the air. Pedaling along the lakefront, Cliff came to the top of a hill and shifted into a higher gear.

On his left, small boats were coming in for the night. On his right, lights were beginning to go on in the windows of the tall buildings facing Lake Shore Drive.

The breeze picked up a bit, and the slight chill reminded Cliff that summer vacation had only a few hours left to it. He hunched down and pedaled harder, as though this might force the fact from his mind.

Not that the summer had been his idea of paradise. Like his last three summers, this one had been kind of lonely. But even a lonely summer vacation was a relief from the pressure of the teachers at Southside Academy.

Besides, to Cliff, lonely was pretty much the way things usually went. He hadn't had any close friends at Southside. He didn't expect to make any at the new school either. That was just the way things were.

He shifted into tenth gear to make the last part of his ride as strenuous as possible. He turned right at the next intersection and headed away from the lake and toward the hotel.

He had two-and-a-half miles to go before he would reach the Ambassador East Hotel. He had taken this ride almost every day during the summer, and he knew the exact mileage from any point on the trip.

He also knew the exact mileage between the hotel and his new high school. But he always tried not to think about that.

It was because of his father's new job at the hotel that he was going to a public high school the next day. He remembered the conversation he'd had with his father back in June.

"It's a real break for me," his father had said. "I've been waiting for years for a chance to manage a hotel that size."

"That's great, Dad."

"I know it'll mean changing schools again, Clifford. But I figure you're probably used to that by now."

"Right, Dad. It's no big deal."

Cliff slowed down until a traffic light ahead of him turned green. Then he picked up his speed again.

It really *isn't* a big deal, he thought. This'll be my eighth school. If I can't handle it by now, I ought to throw in the towel.

The transferring had started five years earlier, when his mother died. His father went from hotel to hotel, always moving up to a better job or a better hotel.

And so they moved. From Boston to Atlanta. From Atlanta to Cleveland. From Cleveland to New York, then back to Boston again.

And now they were in Chicago, and his father was running a top-flight hotel. One thing Cliff didn't like was that his father was making less money than he had at his last job. That's why Cliff had to leave the Academy for a public school.

"But it's only for a while," his father had said. "Once I prove myself, and the raise comes in, I'll send you to any school you pick."

That was a nice promise. But Cliff decided not even to think about it until he had to . For the time being, what he had to think about was the school he was going to the next morning.

He raced up to the hotel entrance and squeezed his brakes. He hopped off the bike, looked at his watch, and smiled. His time was over three minutes better than last night.

He walked the bike up the curb and headed for the door. Roberto, the doorman, stepped in front of him and grinned.

"Hi, Champ," Roberto said. "I got it." Roberto took the bike and waved to one of the parking attendants. Cliff was about to object, but then thought better of it. Roberto enjoyed treating him like a guest. So did most of the other staff members at the hotel.

"Thanks," Cliff said.

"Any time, Champ," Roberto called as he walked the bike off to the side.

Cliff went through the revolving door into the lobby. It was check-in time for a lot of the guests, and the place was full. When you're the son of the manager, that's good news. Cliff smiled a little and walked up the steps toward his father's office.

Darlene, the hostess, stood at the restaurant entrance with a handful of menus. As Cliff walked by, she put her hand on his head and smiled.

"Hi, Cliffy. Finish your bike ride?"

Cliff could feel his face turning red. He looked up at Darlene and smiled.

3

"Yeah," he said. "Is my dad around?"

"I saw him go into his office a few minutes ago," she said.

"Thanks."

He stopped on his way to the office and looked in at the bar. Before he spotted his grandmother, he heard her voice. It drowned out all the other voices and the piano in the corner.

She was sitting at the bar, talking to a middle-aged couple. Cliff was about to duck past the doorway, but she saw him and waved.

He walked up to the bar. Grandma put her arm around his shoulder and kept talking to the couple.

"When my husband was alive," she was saying, "he was practically *nailed* in front of that TV set. I told him TV is a narcotic."

"It is," the man said between sips of his drink. "It is a drug."

"A drug!" Grandma said, loud enough to make several heads turn in her direction. "There he was, a young fella, only sixty-seven, and his eyes were turning into headlights from all that staring."

Cliff tried to slip free, but she tightened her grasp on his shoulder.

"This is my grandson, Clifford," she said, her voice getting even louder. "Clifford, say hello to the Dumpies from Cincinnati."

"The *Dunphys!*" the woman said.

"Yeah," Grandma said. "He makes those cute little get-well cards, and she writes all the verses."

"Hi," Cliff said, finally managing to get free of Grandma's hand. As he walked away from the bar, he noticed the bartender keeping a

4

close eye on Grandma.

Grandma had a reputation for causing trouble with guests. She had a talent for offending people. She almost never realized she was offending them, but she managed to do it more than anyone else Cliff knew.

He winked at the bartender as he passed him. "Watch out for Mrs. Dumpie," Cliff said. "She may be ready to slam Grandma."

He left the bar and walked down to his father's office. "Lawrence Peache, Manager," the sign read. The door was half opened and Cliff walked in. Mr. Peache was talking on the phone. He nodded Cliff toward a chair and kept talking.

"I know, Stan, I know. Please believe me, Stan, it's under control. I can't do that, Stan! She *is* my mother, after all."

A workman poked his head into the doorway. Mr. Peache looked up and listened to whatever Stan was saying on the other end.

"The wiring in 405 is finished," the workman said. "We'll do 406 tomorrow." He turned to go.

"Wait!" Mr. Peache yelled. "No, not you, Stan. Look, I'll call you back in a few minutes. Right."

He hung up the phone and turned to the workman, who was standing impatiently in the doorway.

"What do you mean tomorrow?" Mr. Peache asked. "When tomorrow?"

The workman shrugged his shoulders. "I don't know," he said. "Maybe after lunch."

"That's too late," Mr. Peache said.

"Too bad. I don't do miracles."

He turned and walked out. Mr. Peache took a step toward the doorway. Roberto came in

5

and stopped him.

"She isn't in the restaurant," Roberto said.

"She's at the bar," Cliff said.

"Alone?" Mr. Peache asked.

"No," Cliff answered. "She's preparing some trouble for a couple from Cincinnati."

Roberto went back to his post, and Cliff followed his father toward the bar. Before they reached it, Mr. Griffith stepped in front of them and smirked.

Mr. Griffith's smile always made Cliff think of the strangest things. Right now, the smirk made him see a crocodile trying to do an impression of a TV talk-show host.

Griffith was his father's assistant. He had come with the hotel. Both men had made their feelings clear from the first day. They hated each other passionately.

"Mr. Peache," Griffith said, showing his teeth, "things are going quite badly. The fourth floor is a disaster area. Senator Moore's suite was mistakenly given to someone else. And a Mrs. Dunphy from Cincinnati claims she was insulted at the bar by an elderly lady. We both know who *that* is."

"Good of you to keep me posted, Griffith," Mr. Peache said. More than anything else, he never wanted Griffith to think the job could rattle him. "I'll take care of the Dunphys and the Senator. You go see to the fourth floor."

"Certainly, sir," Griffith said, this time smiling without baring his teeth. He oozed past Cliff and Mr. Peache and slid down the hall.

Mr. Peache watched him go. Then he sighed and said, "Sorry, Clifford. Duty calls. Go in and have something to eat. I'll join you as soon as I can."

6

Clifford nodded and headed for the kitchen. His father went straight for the bar and his troublemaking grandmother.

On his way to the fourth floor, Griffith stopped in his office. He took a phone directory from his desk drawer.

He turned to the phone numbers of the hotel's home office. His finger ran down the list and stopped at Chief of Operations. The smirk was still on his mouth, but his eyes looked dreamy as he dialed the Chief's number.

Three hours later, Cliff stood in the bathroom in his pajamas, brushing his teeth. He rinsed out his mouth, flicked off the light, and stepped out into the suite.

As he padded toward his bedroom, he heard a sound behind him. He paused only for a split second, then continued walking.

He jumped, just a little, when he heard the next sound.

"EEEEEEEEEEEE!" Grandma screeched. "Bat attack! Bat attack!"

He laughed as she smacked him over and over on the back of the head with a rolled-up newspaper.

Finally, she let up, out of breath. "Bat attack," she said, panting. "You okay? I didn't mean to scare you so much."

"You didn't scare me," he said grinning. "I saw you coming."

"You did not!" she yelled, hitting him again with the paper. "Nobody ever suspects a bat attack!"

He reached over and took a pillow from the bed. As she swung the paper, he swung the pillow.

7

"I quit!" she said, throwing the paper in the air. "I give up, you dirty, rotten kid. Hitting an old woman like that."

Grinning, Cliff dropped the pillow and sat on his bed. She sat next to him and caught her breath.

"Oh, look," she said, "I got something for you."

She picked up a large paper bag from the floor and emptied its contents on his bed. "Look at this," she said. "Notebooks, loose-leaf paper, pencils, pens, erasers. I used to love the first day of school."

Cliff smiled at her. "Thanks, Grandma," he said.

The front door opened and closed. She rolled her eyes toward the ceiling.

"Mother?" Mr. Peache called out. "Mother, where are you?"

She looked up meekly as he stepped into the bedroom. He took a deep breath, put his hands on his hips, and began his sermon.

"Mother," he said, as though talking to a child, "I don't own this hotel. I only manage it."

"Don't underrate yourself," she said. "Where would this place be without you?"

"With a new manager, that's where," he said. "Griffith has been watching me like a vulture."

"That greasy little wimp," she spat out.

"Maybe so," he said, "but he's after my job. And you're giving him what he needs to get it."

"I'm sorry," she said, her eyes staring at the carpet. "It won't happen again."

That kind of thing always took the steam

out of her son. He sighed again, almost ready to apologize himself.

"I have to get back to work," he said. "Everything ready for school tomorrow, Clifford?"

"Yep," Cliff said.

"Good. Roberto will be waiting for you at eight. Mother?"

"Yes, Larry?"

"Try—please, try—to act your age."

"If I acted my age," she said, "I'd have been dead years ago."

She laughed. Cliff joined in, and so did her son. It wasn't a bad way to end a summer vacation.

CHAPTER 2

The long, shiny, black Cadillac inched its way along the street, which was crowded with school buses and double-parked cars. The car was the hotel's limousine, used mostly to carry guests to and from the airport.

Cliff had wanted to take the bus, but his father had insisted that Roberto drive him to school and pick him up at the end of the day.

Cliff looked out the window at groups of students standing in front of stores or walking slowly toward school. His gaze ran up and down both sides of the street. Nowhere did he see a student standing or walking alone. They were all in groups.

Par for the course, he thought. This was pretty much the way it was on every opening day. It didn't usually change much throughout the year, either.

"Why don't I get out here, Roberto?" he said. "I can walk faster than we're moving."

"Your father said door-to-door," Roberto said. He looked at Cliff, then took a quick glance at some of the kids outside the car.

"On the other hand," he said grinning, "fathers have been known to be wrong from time to time."

He stopped the car. Cliff picked up his books and opened his door.

"Thanks, Roberto."

"Knock 'em dead, Champ. See you at three-thirty."

Cliff closed the door gently, but it still made enough noise to cause several kids to turn and look. He pretended not to notice as they gaped at his chauffeur-driven limo. He hurried down the block and into the school.

What he noticed first was the noise. Without ever really thinking about it, he thought of school as a relatively quiet place. Quiet was not the order of the day in this building.

Metal locker doors clanged open and shut on both sides of him. Kids called out to other kids in voices he associated with a baseball field.

In the same voices, various teachers yelled directions to nobody in particular. Buried somewhere amid all this sound, a public address system mumbled something about the gym and the cafeteria.

Cliff saw a sign that said *Main Office* and followed the arrow. Near the office, a boy, smaller than himself, was drinking from a water fountain. A tall boy walked up behind him.

The tall boy had black, greasy hair combed straight back and flat on top of his head. He wore faded jeans and a red T-shirt. The shirt was tight enough to make his biceps look bigger than they probably were. His smirk reminded Cliff instantly of Griffith.

Two other boys, dressed in the same kind of clothes, stood behind him. He walked up to the smaller boy and pushed his head into the gurgling fountain.

The boy gasped, pulled away, and looked up. The big guy smiled at him. The boy wiped

11

his wet face on his sleeve. Then he turned and hurried down the hall.

The big guy laughed. His two friends laughed. Then they ambled slowly forward. Cliff passed them on his way into the office. He stared at the big guy, who didn't even notice him.

A half-hour later, he stood in front of his homeroom. The noise hadn't let up for a second, except for the time he'd spent in the main office. He pushed the door of his homeroom open a bit. It was louder in there than anything he'd run into yet.

The yelling was done mostly across the room. It looked as though they had all made a point of sitting as far as possible from people they wanted to talk to. The desks were moveable, so there was a lot of heavy scraping along the floor. One kid in the front used the top of his desk to keep time with music that seemed to exist only in his head.

A woman stood in front of the room, calmly writing on the blackboard. Cliff walked along the wall to the back of the room as the homeroom bell rang.

"Please take any seat," the woman said to the blackboard. She must have known most of them couldn't hear her. She didn't seem to care.

From the back of the room, Cliff looked at the board. "Welcome to Homeroom 10-6 and English 204," it said. "I am your teacher, Ms. Clarice Jump."

Ms. Jump turned to face the class. "Find a seat you like," she said. "You're going to be in it for the rest of the year."

Cliff spotted an empty seat behind a girl in

a green sweater. He moved toward it. She turned and looked up at him.

"I'm saving that for someone," she said.

He saw another empty seat. It was next to the kid who had had his face pushed into the fountain. Cliff sidled over and slipped into the seat.

"Is this saved?" he asked the boy.

"No," the boy said. His eyes darted back and forth between Cliff and other people in the room. He seemed to be expecting something terrible to happen.

"Feel under the desk," he said to Cliff.

Clifford slipped his hand under the desk. He made a face, pulling his hand away, and wiping it on his pants.

The boy's eyes darted toward Cliff again. "You have gum there that dates back to the cavemen," he said. "I'm Willy Carson."

"Hi. Cliff Peache."

"You can get hepatitis from that gum, you know."

Ms. Jump had started calling the roll. Suddenly, the door flew open and two boys stepped in. They were the ones who were laughing when Willy had his face pushed into the water.

"And now," one of them said, "he-e-e-e-re's Moody!'

The girl in the green sweater and some others applauded as Moody stepped in. Moody was the face-pusher.

"Don't applaud," he said, holding his hands in the air, "just throw money." He bowed toward the teacher's desk. "Howdy, ma'am," he said.

"Move it," Ms. Jump said. "To the back."

Moody and his two friends strutted down an aisle toward the back.

"Just my luck," Willy whispered to Cliff. "With all the tenth-grade homerooms, he has to get in mine."

Cliff turned and watched Moody do his act. He slapped the hands of several people as he made his way to the back. The girl in green smiled up at him as he approached her seat.

"I saved you a seat," she said.

He smirked at her. "Good for you, Shelley. Dubrow, you sit there."

One of his two friends took the empty seat. Shelley turned red and looked down at her desk.

Ms. Jump was out in the hall, talking to the assistant principal. Moody turned and noticed Cliff staring at him. Willy hid his eyes.

Moody walked over to Cliff, who continued to stare. "You're sitting in my seat," he said.

Ms. Jump, coming back in, said, "Will you please find a seat back there?"

"I had one," Moody said, not taking his eyes off Cliff. "This goon swiped it."

"I was here first," Cliff said nervously.

"Bull!" Moody yelled.

"Moody!" Ms. Jump said. "Watch how you talk to people. And take that empty seat right there."

He turned and looked at the seat she was pointing to. He motioned to Dubrow, who got up and took the empty seat. Then Moody sat behind Shelley.

"You've got nerve," Willy whispered. "Too bad you aren't going to live long."

Ms. Jump went on with the roll call. "Ricky Linderman," she said.

14

No one answered to the name. But several people gasped and exchanged whispered comments.

"I thought he was still in jail," a girl said.

"Didn't he break a teacher's leg?" a boy asked.

"No," a girl said. "He killed a cop."

Cliff leaned over toward Willy. "Who's Ricky Linderman?" he asked.

"No one," Willy said, looking sad, frightened, and hopeless all at once. "Just the school's mass murderer."

Ms. Jump asked, "Does anyone know if Ricky Linderman is in school today?"

"No," Moody called out. "He's probably in New York, climbing the Empire State Building."

When the laughter died down, Ms. Jump went on with the roll.

"Clifford, uh, P-E-A-C-H-E," she said. "Is Clifford here?" Cliff raised his hand.

"Is that Peach or Peachy?" she asked.

"Clifford Peachpit," Moody said, throwing an angry look at Cliff.

"What was that, Melvin?" Ms. Jump said.

He turned the angry look on her. "I don't use that name any more, Clarice," he said.

"Okay," she said. "You call me Ms. Jump. And what shall we call you?"

"M," he said. "Double-M is good too."

"M & M," Cliff said. "Good stuff for little kids."

The laughter from the class felt good. The look he got from Moody didn't.

Ms. Jump started handing out textbooks. Moody leaned over the desk between him and Cliff.

"You and me, *Clifford*," he said. "We are gonna have a talk after school. Right?"

Cliff stared at him, but didn't answer. He swallowed hard after Moody turned away. He turned to see Willy holding his head in both his hands.

"Ohhhh," Willy moaned. "Boy, are you gonna get it!"

CHAPTER 3

Biology lab was the last class of the day. Science labs were Cliff's all-time favorite school activity. So Cliff busied himself with the fish tank. Moody couldn't have been further from his thoughts.

Willy had no intention of letting that be. He kept up a constant chatter about Moody's past record and Cliff's short time left on this earth.

Cliff had managed to ignore it through most of the day. But now they were working side by side, and Willy's monologue was beginning to penetrate.

"That was so dumb, what you did this morning," Willy said. "I never saw anybody put Moody down before. I hope you get away with it. But, of course, you won't."

Cliff looked from the fish to Willy. He pointed to a small hose on the table.

"We can use that hose to fill the other tank," he said.

Willy handed him the hose. "Just don't let him get you in the halls alone," he said. "Or on the stairs."

Cliff rigged up the hose to run water through a filter into the tank. He began putting gravel into the tank.

"Or near any of the side exits," Willy went on. "Or the bathrooms. Especially in the bathrooms. I never go to the bathroom in this building."

Cliff looked up from his work. "What do you do?" he asked.

"Develop self-discipline," Willy said sadly. "Also, stay away from liquids."

Cliff smiled at him. "That's ridiculous," he said.

"You think so, huh?" Willy said, getting excited. "They say one kid got thrown out a window last year. A *bathroom* window! They say he's a vegetable now!"

Cliff said, "That's dumb, Willy. Who told you that?"

"Plenty of people! Then there's this other guy, who had his eye kicked out. Totally gross. They never found the eyeball."

Cliff kept working, but he wasn't smiling now. "Moody did that?" he asked.

Suddenly, Willy sounded like a reluctant witness in a courtroom. "I'm not saying he did, and I'm not saying he didn't. But from my point of view, it's better to pay him the protection money."

"You pay Moody for protection?"

"You better believe it," Willy said. "Lots of kids do. I figure he's about a billionaire by now. He takes our lunch money every day. So I started bringing lunch this year. Now he says he's gonna take my bus fare."

Cliff stared at him. Willy showed a weak smile.

"Oh, well," he said, his voice cracking a little. "I can use the exercise."

"I don't think you should let him get away with it," Cliff said.

"Yeah, I know," Willy said. "But you see, I have this problem. I'm addicted to breathing."

The final bell rang at two-thirty. Cliff and

18

Willy finished putting away the equipment they'd been working with and picked up their books.

"See ya," Cliff said.

"Good-bye," Willy said solemnly. "It's been nice knowing you."

He turned and walked off. Cliff watched him go. He smiled a little and shook his head. Then he followed Willy out of the room.

The halls were noisy, but not as bad as they were in the morning. Cliff made his way through small knots of students toward the stairway.

He bounced down the stairs that led to the front entrance. He stopped halfway down when he saw Moody near the door. Dubrow and Hightower, his two goons, were on either side of him. All three smiled at Cliff.

Cliff turned and went back up the stairs. For the first time, he began to think seriously about what Willy had been saying all day long.

For a second, that funny feeling in the pit of his stomach was unfamiliar. Then he recognized it. It was fear.

He had to think hard to remember the last time he'd had that feeling. It was years before, one night when he was walking home alone long after dark.

He'd stayed late to work on a science project. He was supposed to get a ride home with a kid in his class, but they got their signals crossed. He wound up walking the ten blocks.

Nothing had happened that night. Nobody stopped him, or even noticed him, as far as he could remember. But he was scared all the same.

Now, here it was again, that feeling that hit your stomach, your knees, and your head, all at the same time. There was a difference this time, though. This time, he knew what there was to be afraid of.

He reached the top of the stairs and went straight for the library. A sign on the door told him it closed at three-thirty.

The librarian was working at her desk. No one else was there. He put his books on a table and sat down. He hadn't been running, but he was having trouble catching his breath.

He knew he was safe for the time being. Moody and Co. wouldn't start anything with the librarian here. All he had to do was keep an eye on the window. With Roberto at the front entrance, Moody would have to back off.

By three-twenty, Cliff was nearly in a frenzy. He'd already pretended to look through every magazine in the librarian's rack. He'd faked it with a couple of books from the shelves. Now she was packing her stuff away, getting ready to leave.

He stared at the magazine in front of him. Then he heard her walking up behind him.

"Excuse me," she said. He looked up at her. "I'm going to lock up in a few minutes. Is there anything I can help you with?"

"No," Cliff said, "no thanks." He gathered his books together, not able to think of any way of stretching his stay here.

Then he heard the car horn. He ran for the window and looked out. The limo had never looked so beautiful. He turned and smiled at the librarian.

"See ya," he said, and walked out of the library.

He trotted to the stairs and took them three at a time. His eyes were on the floor as he hit the first floor landing. What he saw was four other feet facing him. He looked up and saw Dubrow and Hightower staring at him menacingly.

"What have we here?" Dubrow said. Each of them grabbed one of his arms.

"We're having a little party after school," Hightower said. "And you're the guest of honor, Peachy."

He struggled, but they were too strong for him. They half-carried, half-pushed him into the boys' room near the entrance. Inside, Moody had a ninth-grader pinned to the wall. The kid was crying.

"Hey, Moody!" Dubrow said. "We got a present for you!"

"Wait a minute," Moody said, without turning around. "That's two dollars tomorrow," he said to the kid. "And a dollar a day from now on. Every day. Got it?"

"Yeah," the kid said, sobbing. "I got it."

"Good," Moody said, backing away from him. "Now beat it."

The kid looked grateful as he picked up his books and scampered out the door. Moody turned to face Cliff.

"Well," he said. "If it isn't Peachpit."

He held out his hand. Cliff backed away.

"Hey," Moody said, "I'm just trying to be friends."

His hand was still out. Cliff looked from him to Dubrow, then to Hightower. Then he looked back at Moody's hand. He reached out, and they shook hands.

"That's better," Moody said, putting his arm

21

around Cliff. "Where did you go to school before you came here, man?"

Cliff's stomach was doing somersaults, and he wasn't sure his knees were going to continue to support his weight. But he was determined not to let it show.

"Southside Academy," he said.

"Ohhh, private school," Hightower said. "You rich?"

"No," Cliff said.

"Somebody saw you come to school in a Caddy this morning," Dubrow said.

"It belongs to the hotel my father works at," Cliff said.

"Look, Peachfuzz," Moody said, "it's obvious you got bread. The question is, have you got sense?" When he got no response, he said, "I'm asking have you got sense?"

"I think so," Cliff said. "Sometimes."

"I think so too," Moody said.

Hightower took a roll of toilet paper from a stall. He tore off large pieces and rolled them in wads. Then he started wetting the wads.

"Because you got sense," Moody said, "you know this is not like those private academies you're used to."

WHACK! Hightower had tossed a wad of wet paper at the ceiling. It was stuck there, water dripping from it to the floor.

"You go to a school like this," Moody said, "you need a bodyguard. I mean, you wouldn't believe some of the things that go on here."

WHACK! Another wad was stuck to the ceiling.

"Hey," Hightower said, "you know we got Linderman in our homeroom?"

"Peachpit," Moody said, "you know about

Linderman? He's psycho, man, totally freaked out. He wasted some kid. Shot him right in the head. Blew his brains out!"

WHACK! WHACK!

"Why did he do that?" Cliff asked. He spoke slowly, to try to hide his nervousness.

"Probably no reason at all," Moody said. "Guys like Linderman, they just lose control, you know?"

"AAAAAARRRRRRRGGGGGGHHHHH!" Dubrow screamed, to show how guys like that lose control.

"That's when you come to us," Moody said. "We're bodyguards. Interested?" Cliff didn't answer, and Moody went on. "A buck a day. We give everybody the same deal. You can pay day-to-day, or by the week."

"Where am I gonna get a dollar every day?" Cliff asked.

"Lunch money," Moody said. "That stuff they serve is garbage anyway."

"I'm not giving you my lunch money, "Cliff said. "I have to eat."

"Oh," Moody said. The false-friendly tone was still in his voice.

One of the wet wads of toilet paper had peeled itself from the ceiling and fallen to the floor. Moody went over and picked it up.

"Tell you what," he said. "Eat this."

He held the wet paper up toward Cliff's face. Cliff backed away.

"It beats cafeteria food," Moody said. He stepped toward Cliff, who kept moving back.

As Moody advanced, the toilet paper extended, Cliff heard a car horn. It was *the* car horn. Roberto gave it a couple of long toots.

It was now or never. If Cliff didn't get out

there, Roberto might think he'd gone home on his own. He'd have to get out there *now*.

Moody took another step, an evil grin on his face. He waved the wet toilet paper in front of Cliff's face. Hightower and Dubrow stood against the far wall, laughing.

Cliff stopped. Moody took another step, then another. Cliff reached up and grabbed the extended hand.

Before Moody could tighten his arm, Cliff had doubled it over toward his face. He pushed the elbow, and Moody's hand jammed his own mouth full of wet toilet paper.

Moody's eyes widened, and his face took on a disgusting look. Hightower and Dubrow were still laughing. They didn't know what had happened until he turned to face them.

Even then, it took them several seconds to believe what they saw. Moody stood there, looking sickly, his arms extended in their direction. The wet paper hung from his mouth, sticking to his chin and the front of his shirt. He began spitting it out.

Cliff was already out the door and heading for the front entrance. He reached it and threw his weight against it. It was locked.

The three of them were out of the bathroom now, right behind him. He charged up the stairs and ran down the hall, desperately looking for a way out.

He didn't even know where the exits were in this building. Even if he found one, he wouldn't know if it was locked until he reached it. He ran down the hallway, beginning to pant.

Three sets of footsteps were close behind. Up ahead, he saw a classroom door standing open. He ran for it, got inside, and closed the door behind him.

He got on the other side of the teacher's desk and pushed it toward the door. It was heavy, and the going was very, very, slow. But he jammed it against the door before they reached it.

They pushed on the door, but the desk was too heavy. He saw Moody's face in the little window in the middle of the door. It was ugly, filled with hate. Moody pounded on the door.

"Come on out, Peachpit!" he screamed. "You gotta come out sometime! We can wait!"

Cliff went to the window. There was the limo, right below him. There was only one thing to do.

He opened the window and climbed on the sill. The pounding on the door stopped.

"He's going out the window!" Dubrow shouted.

Roberto tooted the horn. Cliff climbed out on the ledge and looked down. It wasn't nearly as bad as he thought it would be. He closed his eyes and jumped.

He hit the ground feet first, fell forward, and rolled. His feet were stinging, and he scraped his knee.

He picked up his books and ran for the car. When he opened the door, Roberto looked up.

"Oh, there you are," he said pleasantly. "I thought I'd missed you."

"Let's go," Cliff said.

Moody, Hightower, and Dubrow came running out of a side door. They ran for the car as Roberto took off.

"What's going on?" Roberto asked. "Who are those guys?"

Breathing heavily, Cliff said, "Just some guys I met at school."

"Oh," Roberto said.

"They want to kill me," Cliff added.

Roberto grinned at him and shook his head.

"Kids," he said philosophically.

CHAPTER 4

Cliff leaned on the railing of his terrace, looking out over Chicago. It was a warm night, even though the breeze was beginning to pick up. Grandma sat behind him on a lounge chair. She was reading the racing form.

Both his ankles were sore from the jump he'd made. The scrape on his knee wasn't too bad, but he'd had to throw away his pants because of the hole in the leg.

He watched a plane slowly circling overhead, waiting for its turn to land at the airport.

"They want to kill me," he'd told Roberto. He wondered just how much of an exaggeration that really was.

How much truth was there in the stories Willy had told him? What would Moody and his goons do when they got their chance? How crazy were they really?

He kept seeing the face of Moody looking through the small window in the classroom door. There was fury in those eyes. There was hatred, and there was cruelty. Maybe it wasn't the face of a crazy person. But it would do, until something worse came along.

Grandma was saying something, but he didn't know what it was. It took him a few seconds to pull himself away from that horrible face.

"What?" he asked.

"I said who do you like in the fourth tomorrow?"

"Lucky Lou," Cliff said absently.

"Clifford!" she snapped. "This is a science we're dealing with, not guesswork!"

Cliff turned at the sound of footsteps. His father came out on the terrace. He looked very tired.

"Mother," Mr. Peache said, "I have an idea. Why don't we just pack up and leave? We can go on welfare."

"Have a mint," she said, smiling and holding out a small dish.

"Where were you at five o'clock?" he asked, ignoring the peace offering.

"Five o'clock?" she said. "Let me see. Oh, yes, I was having a drink at the bar."

"Yes," he said. "And you were trying to interest some guy in your latest system for the horses. It happens the man is a preacher."

"No wonder he looked so serious."

"You think he looked serious? You should have seen Griffith after the guy complained. I think Griffith is keeping a written record of all your more exciting adventures around here. I have a pretty good idea who's going to get to read it."

She smiled at him and went back to her racing form. He sighed and shook his head. Then he went over to Cliff and put his arm around him.

"Roberto said you had a little trouble with some kids today," he said.

"Yeah," Cliff said. He smiled a little, trying to make it seem like nothing.

"Well, don't you worry about it," Grandma said. "Your dad already called and raised a stink about it."

"You called the *school*?" Cliff gasped.

"The principal was gone for the day," Mr.

Peache said. "But I managed to get his home phone number."

"Oh, great!" Cliff said, falling into a chair. "Now I'll really get slaughtered!"

"You won't get slaughtered, Clifford," his father said.

"They already think I'm a nerd."

"Clifford," his father said, "the principal is going to talk to those boys and straighten this all out. They won't bother you again."

"That's what you think," Cliff said.

"If they try anything," Grandma said, "you go right for the eye." She made a fist and punched at the air. "Hard as you can. Blinds 'em. You gotta get in the first punch."

"Mother!" Mr. Peache said. "There are other ways of handling things. I don't think he can solve this with his fists."

"Right," she said. "There's a lot to be said for a well-placed kick too."

Cliff slid down in his chair and tried to imagine what his second day of school was going to be like.

Moody didn't show up for homeroom, so Cliff didn't see him until third period. That's when he was told to report to the principal's office.

Moody was waiting when Cliff got there. He was sitting on a bench outside the office. He stared at Cliff, with no expression at all.

The secretary came out and led them inside. Mr. Rath was on the phone. The secretary left, closing the door behind her.

He was about 50, a big man, maybe a former football player. His suit was rumpled, his tie was crooked, and the top button of his shirt was open. Cliff liked him right away.

He hung up the phone and said, "Mr. Moody

and Mr. Peache. Well, Moody, you didn't waste any time this year, did you?"

"I didn't do nothing," Moody said.

"All right, Clifford," Mr. Rath said, "what did they take from you?"

"Didn't take nothing," Moody said.

"You zip it up, Mister," he snapped at Moody. "Clifford, how much?"

"Well," Cliff said, "they didn't actually take anything."

"Nothing?" Mr. Rath said. He seemed disappointed, and Cliff thought about apologizing.

"Nothing, sir," Moody said. "We were only kidding him."

"I'll determine that," Rath said, "not you. Now, Clifford, they didn't get your money. But they harmed you in some way?"

"No, but —"

"Oh, man," Moody said, "can I say something?"

"You simmer down," Rath said. "You'll have your chance to speak."

"Please, Mr. Rath?" Moody said. "I can prove we were joking."

That seemed to catch Rath's interest. It caught Cliff's too. How was Moody going to prove something like that?

"Go ahead," Rath said.

"Look," Moody said, "I'm no saint, right? Don't you think I could whip this dude if I really wanted to?"

"You don't whip anybody," Rath said, sitting up to his full height. "Not around here, you don't."

"I know, I know," Moody said. "but give me credit. If I *wanted* to trash him, I'd have done

30

it. You know that. That's how I can prove we were just putting him on. Because I *didn't* touch him. But the kid can't even take a joke, you know?"

"I don't see the humor in extortion," Mr. Rath said, "real or pretended. There is nothing funny about extortion."

"Okay, okay," Moody said. "I admit it backfired."

He did it! Cliff thought. He was going to get away with it.

"You bet it backfired," Mr. Rath said. "On you. I ought to suspend you. But since there was no real harm done, I'm going to be a nice guy. I'll let you off with a week's detention. Just consider yourself lucky. Take a walk."

Moody had been holding a humble-serious look during Mr. Rath's final speech. As he turned to walk out, his regular sneer came back. He grinned at Cliff and left.

"Clifford," Mr. Rath said, "it takes time to adjust to a new school. Things here are less sheltered than at Southside. But try not to let that throw you. Just don't sound the alarm every time somebody looks cross-eyed at you. Okay, son?" Cliff nodded. "All right. Go back to class."

Cliff's feelings were really confused as he left the office. He was relieved that nothing serious had happened. He was also angry that Moody could get away with things as easily as he had.

He saw Mr. Rath as a decent guy who was trying to be strict and fair at the same time. He also saw him as a jerk who could be easily conned by Moody's fast talk.

He turned a corner to go up the stairs and

ran smack into Moody, standing on the first step, his hands in his back pockets. He glared down at Cliff.

"You're giving me trouble," Moody said slowly. "People don't do that around here."

Cliff took a step back. Moody stepped down and toward him.

"You better grow eyes in the back of your head, Peachpit. Because that's the only way you're gonna know when it's coming."

Cliff took another step back, staring into Moody's eyes. Moody lifted his right hand to shoulder level and made a fist. He fired it toward Cliff's face and stopped just short of hitting him.

Cliff reflexively pulled his head back from the oncoming fist.

When the fist stopped in midair, Moody laughed and winked at him. Then he turned and walked off down the hall.

Cliff swallowed the anger and the embarrassment. He didn't know what else to do with it.

There was only one piece of good news from the whole incident. Moody had a week's detention. That meant Cliff could safely get out of the school for the next five days.

The next morning, Ms. Jump was introducing *Romeo and Juliet*. That is, she was trying to find a way of convincing the class that they really did want to read the play, no matter what they thought.

"You see," she was saying, "this guy Shakespeare is a pretty cool guy. The play is about love, and sex, and gang wars, and blood. Just like *West Side Story*, only the language is poetry. Are you interested?"

The class broke into loud laughter. Ms. Jump was about to call for silence. But the silence came immediately—and totally—before she could even raise her hand. She saw everyone staring at the front door, and she slowly turned her head to look.

Willy leaned over to fill Cliff in on the latest disaster. "It's Linderman!" he whispered.

The name was being whispered all over the room. The object of everybody's attention stood near the door and let it slam shut behind him.

Could this really be a high school student, Cliff wondered. From where he sat, Linderman looked about seven feet tall and seemed to weigh 250 pounds. His baggy pants made Cliff wonder if they could have once belonged to somebody even bigger.

He was wearing a grubby army field jacket. He needed a haircut and a shave. Maybe even a leash, Cliff thought. A very strong leash. Linderman looked around the room and scowled.

"Hello, Ricky," Ms. Jump said softly. "Do you have a pass?"

Linderman looked at her, then down at his hand. Sure enough, it held a little white piece of paper. He held it out to her.

She walked over and took it from him.She read it and said, "Fine. There's a seat right here in the front, if you want it."

He scanned the room again and spotted two empty seats in the back. One was right behind Willy. The other was on the opposite side of the room.

"Please let him take the other seat." Willy whispered.

Cliff watched Linderman make his way to

the back. He moved awkwardly, like a truck with a couple of flat tires. People lowered their eyes as he walked past. But he didn't notice. His attention was on the back of the room.

"Please don't let him come over here!" Willy whispered, holding his head.

Linderman reached the back of the room. He walked past the first empty chair.

"He's coming this way!" Willy whispered. "I knew it! I knew I'd never get out of the tenth grade alive!"

Cliff turned to watch Linderman walk along the back of the room. Everyone else, including Moody, Dubrow, and Hightower, stared stonily at the front of the room.

"Right in back of me," Willy said, almost out loud. "I'll have a heart attack."

Linderman stood next to the empty seat behind Willy. He was big. But Cliff was relieved to see that he wasn't a giant, after all. Just a big guy who could crack you in two if you got him angry.

He lowered himself into the seat. Cliff had visions of a crane being brought into the classroom to make the operation easier.

Once seated, he looked at the only kid who was facing him. When their eyes met, Cliff saw something he didn't understand. For a second, they didn't look like the eyes of a killer. For a second, Cliff almost thought he saw the beginnings of a smile in Linderman's eyes.

But it was gone so quickly that Cliff wasn't sure he'd seen it at all. All he saw now was the unshaven face of a big, hulking creature. Willy's tales about Linderman didn't seem at all farfetched.

Cliff turned to face the front of the room. The silence was so complete that the shuffling of his feet sounded like a kettle drum.

"All right," Ms. Jump said uncertainly. "Now that we're all settled down, let's get back to work. Ricky, we're talking about *Romeo and Juliet*."

Linderman stared straight ahead at the empty blackboard.

CHAPTER 5

After lunch, Cliff went to the locker room to change for gym. He was alone because Willy had gone home sick after English class. The shock of Linderman's arrival had proved too much for him.

Cliff had seen Linderman eating in the cafeteria. When Linderman came in, all heads turned toward him, just as they had in the classroom. He sat at a table with eight chairs. Seven of them remained empty until he left.

Cliff changed into his gym suit and left his books and clothes in the locker. In the gym, Moody, Hightower, Dubrow, and a few others were playing something. It was a mixture of basketball, volleyball, and boxing.

Cliff stood in the doorway and watched. Linderman and another boy, both fully dressed, sat on a bench on the sidelines. A whistle blew, and Mr. Dorfman, the gym teacher, came out of his office bouncing a basketball.

"All right," he yelled. "Off the courts, let's go!"

He took the basketball from Dubrow. Cliff joined the crowd standing in front of Dorfman. He split them up into groups of five, with Moody, Hightower, and Dubrow in one group.

Then he noticed Linderman and the other boy sitting on the bench. He walked over to them, bouncing the basketball as he moved.

"What do we have here?" Dorfman said.

"Visiting dignitaries? What's the matter with you guys?"

The other boy held up his left arm to show his cast. "It comes off next week," he said.

Dorfman nodded, then looked at Linderman. "And what about you?"

Linderman stared at him.

"Are you deaf?" Dorfman said, his voice tense with anger.

Linderman stared. Dorfman dropped the basketball and let it roll away. He moved his feet to plant them more solidly and put his hands on his hips.

"Stand up, mister," he said through his teeth.

Linderman lumbered to his feet, never once looking away from Dorfman's eyes. He stood almost a full head over Dorfman. They looked like a couple of tanks facing each other.

"What's your name?" Dorfman said slowly All he got was a stare. "I'm only going to ask once more, mister. What's your name?"

The gym was so silent it didn't matter that the answer was mumbled. Everyone heard it.

"Linderman."

From behind, Cliff could see Dorfman's shoulders tighten a little. He turned and blew his whistle.

"Okay," he yelled. "Let's play ball."

Cliff stood staring at Linderman. Their eyes met for a second, and he saw it again. Some-thing—almost a smile in the eyes, but gone too quickly for him to be sure it was really there.

Cliff took the court with four other boys against Moody's team. Cliff got the tipoff and dribbled toward the basket.

He moved into the foul circle and Moody's elbow sank deep into his ribs. He fell to the floor in pain, trying to catch his breath. He opened his eyes to see Moody standing over him.

"Watch the rough stuff, will ya?" Moody said, smiling. "It's only a game."

Cliff got up and looked at the bench. The boy with the cast was doing his homework. Linderman was gone. Cliff watched the gym door slowly swing closed.

Thirty minutes later, Cliff found the lock on his locker broken. He opened the door. His books and clothes were buried under a pile of rotten bananas, peaches, and plums.

He picked his stuff from the locker, trying to keep from smearing the fruit more than it already was. As he knelt there, Dubrow walked past him.

"If I were you," Dubrow said, "I'd report that to the principal."

The laughter from Moody and Hightower followed him out of the room. He went to the boys' bathroom in his gym suit, carrying his dirty clothes.

He tried washing them in the sink, but without much luck. Then he heard voices coming from the hall outside. One of them belonged to Moody.

He collected all his stuff and moved for the stalls. One of them was being used. He moved down two stalls, slipped inside, and locked the door. Then he stood on the toilet seat, so his feet wouldn't show at the bottom of the door.

Balancing himself with one hand against the wall, he held his books and clothes in the other hand. He hid there, listening to Moody and Dubrow over near the sinks.

"She's already crazy about me," Moody said.

"No kidding?" Dubrow said.

"She looked in my eyes in homeroom. She saw a guy who's got it together. She saw a man in control, a guy with power. Women go for that, you know."'

"She sees the power," Dubrow said.

"Damn right," Moody said.

Cliff listened to the footsteps. They went from the sinks to the door. He heard the door swing open, then slam shut. He counted to ten. Then he stepped off the seat, unlocked the door, and slid out of the stall.

"Hi," Moody grinned, as he leaned against the door.

"Small world, ain't it?" Dubrow added.

Moody folded his arms and nodded toward Dubrow. "My accountant here says there's something overdue on the books from you."

"Right," Dubrow said.

"Look," Cliff said. "I'm not going to pay. That's it. So do what you have—"

Moody took a step toward him, but stopped at the sound of a flushing toilet. The door of the other stall opened. Linderman stepped out.

Moody's face was pale. "Let's get something to eat," he said.

He and Dubrow hurried out the door. Cliff turned and saw Linderman washing his hands at a sink. He looked again at the exit where Moody and Dubrow had just run out like a couple of scared rabbits. Then he looked back at Linderman.

Linderman dried his hands on a paper towel and walked past Cliff without looking at him. Cliff stood alone in the bathroom. He was smiling.

"Why not?" he said out loud. "Why not?"

He waited for him after last period. Linderman had no locker because he didn't carry any books, so he was one of the first people out the door. Cliff saw him light up a cigarette and step outside. He ran and caught up with him.

"Excuse me," Cliff called.

Linderman walked in long strides, his hands buried deep in the pockets of his field jacket. Cliff ran a little faster.

"Linderman? Could you wait a minute?"

The strides seemed to get longer, the hands went deeper into the pockets, and Linderman's shoulders went up. Cliff picked up speed.

"Linderman! Could I ask you a question?"

He caught up with him and kept trotting along. Linderman glanced at him for a second, then turned away. The pace never slowed.

"Just a couple of seconds," Cliff said. "I wouldn't bother you, but it's really important. Okay?"

Linderman stopped. He turned and faced Cliff. This time, Cliff was sure. There was no doubt about it.

Linderman was smiling. Well, *almost* smiling. But it was only in his eyes. It was as though his face muscles hadn't yet learned how to form anything but a scowl. But it was there in the eyes, Cliff was sure of it. Then it was gone again.

"Look," Cliff said, "I hope you won't get mad or anything. But I want to make you an offer."

Linderman stared. Suddenly, Cliff thought he knew how Dorfman must have felt earlier in the gym. It's hard to talk to somebody who not only doesn't answer, but doesn't even show if he understands. Or hears.

"An offer," Cliff repeated, as though maybe Linderman hadn't understood. "See, I was wondering if you'd like to make some money."

Still nothing but a stare. Cliff decided to be optimistic. Linderman hadn't crushed his skull. He took that as a good sign and plunged ahead.

"See, there are these guys. Maybe you noticed them in the bathroom. They're trying to make me pay protection."

"From what?"

He spoke! He actually spoke to me, Cliff thought. He was so giddy at this turn of events, that he didn't answer for a few seconds. At which point, Linderman spoke again.

"Protection from what?"

'Well, from *them*, of course, but that isn't what they say. They *say* they're protecting me—and some of the other kids too—from other people. From—well—mainly—from you."

"From me?"

The face remained stony, but there was something new in the eyes. It wasn't anger, which is what Cliff had expected. It wasn't sadistic amusement, which wouldn't have surprised him.

It was more like puzzlement. Just a few seconds, naturally, and then it was gone.

"That's what they say," Cliff said, adding quickly, "but I know it isn't true. At least I think it isn't true. And that's how I came up with this idea."

"What idea?"

Now there was genuine suspicion in the eyes. The voice seemed to have dropped a couple of stories. Cliff wondered if maybe he wasn't making a terrible mistake.

"Here's my idea," he said. He took a deep breath and went on. "I'll pay you to be my bodyguard. Maybe some of the other kids would too. You could make some good money. Also, I could do your homework. I'm pretty smart, I mean I'm a pretty good student. See, I wouldn't mind paying you, because at least it wouldn't be extortion."

The look was back in the eyes. Only this time, it actually affected the muscles of Linderman's face. What happened to his face couldn't actually be called a smile. But it was clearly a non-scowl. Linderman was amused.

"Not interested," he said. Then he turned and lumbered away.

Cliff turned to go back toward the school and wait for Roberto. Dubrow and Hightower were leaning against a lamppost, looking at him. Both their jaws hung loose.

CHAPTER 6

Except for Cliff and his father, the hotel restaurant was empty. Cliff listened to Grandma singing in the kitchen as she made their breakfast. He stared out the window. His father read the morning paper.

Griffith and Grandma both came into the restaurant together. Grandma carried a tray with three plates of scrambled eggs and bacon. Griffith had an unusual bounce in his step, and he was smiling.

"Good morning, Mrs. Peache," he said loudly. "How are we today?"

Grandma snarled at him and put the tray on the table. Mr. Peache folded his paper and put it on the seat next to him.

"Good morning, Griffith," he said. "Have some eggs."

"No, thank you," he sang. "I just came in to give you a message."

He was too pleased with himself. Mr. Peache realized something was wrong.

"What message?" he asked.

"The home office just called. Mr. Dobbs— the Chief of Operations?—is coming for a visit on Monday."

Mr. Peache's face fell. "Any particular reason?" he asked.

Griffith looked at Grandma and said, "Your guess is as good as mine."

As he walked—danced, really—past the table on his way out, Grandma dropped some

51

scrambled eggs on his shoe.

"So sorry," she said. "Let me get you some water to wipe it off."

"Never mind," Griffith said, his spirits dampened. He stormed into the kitchen.

"What was that all about?" Grandma asked through a mouth full of eggs.

"Guess," Mr. Peache said. He bent over his eggs and began eating.

Cliff pushed his plate away. "I'm too nervous to eat," he said.

"What are you nervous about?" his father asked. "Everything okay at school?"

"Terrific," Cliff said.

"Are you sure? I could call the principal again."

"No! Everything's fine. Everything's just perfect!"

He thought of what he'd told his father at breakfast as he sailed through the air during lunch. He watched his lunch fly away in front of him. The milk hit the floor at the same time he did.

Lying on his stomach, he turned to see Hightower's foot still out in the aisle. Another foot stepped over him. It belonged to Moody.

"You should be more careful," Moody said as he walked away.

Cliff got up and began collecting pieces of the mess. He glanced up and saw Linderman watching him. They looked at each other for a few seconds. Then Linderman got up, picked up his empty tray, and walked out.

Cliff got up early on Saturday, long before his father and grandmother. The beautiful weather boosted his spirits, which were high to begin with. Not having to go to school was enough to send them sailing over the Sears Building.

He had agreed to meet Willy and another kid, Ron, at the park. Willy, small as he was, was into rowing, and Cliff thought it sounded like a good idea.

At the park, Willy insisted on rowing first. So Cliff and Ron set up a chess board and let him have his way.

"I can't believe you really talked to him," Willy grunted as he rowed. "I'm even surprised he speaks any language known to man."

"I only talked to him for a minute," Cliff said. "And he didn't say much."

"What did you talk to him about?" Ron asked.

"Nothing much."

"What do you mean, nothing much?" Willy asked. He rested the oars in the locks. "You don't talk to Linderman about the weather."

"How would you know?" Cliff said, his eyes on the chess board. "You've never talked to him. Where does he hang out? Do you know?"

"Probably the slaughterhouse," Willy said. He got back to his rowing.

"What's the matter with him, anyway?" Cliff asked.

"From what I hear," Ron said, "a number of things. One, he's supposed to have beaten up a woman teacher in front of a whole class. Your move. I also heard he shot a cop."

"I know for a fact," Willy grunted as he rowed, "that what he did was kill a kid. Two years ago. In cold blood. Blew his brains out. Blam!"

Staring at the board, Cliff said, "I don't be-lieve it."

"Look it up, then," Willy said. "It was in the papers."

"Checkmate," Ron said.

Cliff looked up just as they were nearing a small bridge. Shelley was standing there, watching their boat.

Cliff had been staring at Shelley since the first time he'd walked into homeroom. But he knew she was interested in Moody. That was enough to limit him to only staring. He had enough trouble.

As they got closer, he saw that she was look-ing at him. Willy was busy rowing. Ron was setting up the pieces for a new game.

So when she waved, he knew it was meant for him. He waved back, and they passed un-der the bridge. As they moved away from it, he looked up, and she was gone.

On Monday morning, Cliff went to the school library. The librarian was busy with index cards. She looked up, not pleased with the interruption.

"Do you keep back copies of newspapers here?" he asked.

"You'll have to go to the public library for that," she said. "Downtown."

"Thanks," he said.

"What are you looking for?" she asked, lay-ing her index cards down.

"I'm trying to find out about somebody who committed a murder."

"Who's the somebody?"

"It doesn't matter," he said. "It was—uh—just a kid."

"Well," she said, "if it's a minor, you'll have a hard time."

"Why?"

"The police don't release the names of minors."

"Oh," he said, not happy about facing a dead end. "Well, thanks anyway."

Moody and Co. continued their games. Apparently, they'd decided to wear Cliff down little by little, instead of killing him outright. The garbage in his locker; the foot in the aisle in the cafeteria—that was the pattern they were going to follow.

Moody probably figured it was risky to do anything outright. Cliff might go to the principal again. So they did it more subtly.

Cliff was casually roughed up in gym class. He had several small "accidents" in the halls. And his locker was broken into twice more. He finally gave up on it, preferring to carry all his stuff around in a duffel bag.

Once they almost got themselves caught. They were pushing him around on a stairway, when a teacher came up. They ran, but the teacher had already seen what they were doing.

"Who were those boys?" the teacher asked.

"I don't know," Cliff said.

"Are you sure?" the teacher demanded. "They should be suspended for that kind of thing."

"I don't know them," Cliff said. "Excuse me, sir. I'm supposed to be at the pool, and I'm late."

Telling him wouldn't have solved anything. It might have got them suspended. But Cliff needed something more permanent than that.

Willy had already changed into his bathing suit when Cliff got to the locker room. Moody, Dubrow, and Hightower, fully dressed, stood in a semicircle around him.

"Hey, Carson," Moody said, "ain't you been forgetting something lately"

Willy looked terrified. 'N-no," he stammered. "I mean—"

"Then where's my money?"

'Well, I—" Willy swallowed. "I just didn't think I had to pay," he said. "Not when Cliff isn't."

"Is that right?" Moody said. He picked up a towel and walked across the room toward Cliff.

"Did you hear that?" Moody said. Dubrow and Hightower were right behind him now. "Do you see what kind of trouble you're causing me?"

He waited. Cliff stared at him.

"What did you call me?" Moody screamed. "Did you guys hear what he said?"

"Yeah," Hightower said.

"Yeah, we heard," Dubrow added.

Moody tossed the towel over Cliff's head. Cliff dropped his duffel bag and tried to get the towel off. But Moody had grabbed the ends and was tightening it around his neck.

"Can't call me that and get away with it," Moody said.

He slammed Cliff against the lockers, holding the towel tight with one hand. Cliff fell to the floor, the towel still tight around his head.

Moody dragged him along the floor. Cliff kicked and struggled, while he tried to get his head uncovered. Hightower and Dubrow kept pushing his hands away from the towel.

He couldn't get the towel loose. And he couldn't see who he was fighting. Even his yells were muffled. It was as good as being tied and gagged.

Moody pulled him along. His knees and elbows banged into benches and lockers. The dragging finally stopped, and Moody pulled him to his feet.

"Get in there!" he screamed.

As the towel finally came off his head, Cliff saw himself being jammed into one of the narrow lockers. Four of five hands pressed him in. The door slammed shut behind him. Then he heard a lock being slipped through the holes in the frame.

He kicked at the door. He pushed with his hands. Then he tried his shoulders. It seemed ridiculous. He was locked into a locker less than two feet wide.

"Let me out of here!" he yelled. He banged on the door, then pounded with both fists.

"LET ME OUT!" he screamed.

Willy had probably run out the first chance he got. Nobody else had been in the locker room. How long was he going to have to wait? How long *could* he wait?

"LET ME OUT, LET ME OUT!" There was terror in the screams now. He was crying, real tears, crying the way he used to when he was a kid.

How long could they do this kind of thing to him? How long was he supposed to put up with it? Why didn't he just give in and pay them the money? HOW WAS HE GOING TO GET OUT OF THIS LOCKER?

"LET ME OUT!" His pounding was weak

now. Most of his energy was going into the crying.

"LET ME OUT!"

Then he heard footsteps. They were slow and deliberate. Moody coming back, maybe to set fire to the locker?

No, it was one set of footsteps. Moody never traveled alone, especially on business.

"Willy?" Cliff called. "Willy, is that you?"

No answer. It wasn't Willy, and it wasn't Moody. The footsteps came closer. They stopped in front of the locker.

He began pounding again and crying. "Who's out there?" he yelled. "Let me out of here! Whoever you are, let me out!"

A hand reached down and slipped the lock from the holes. Cliff pounded and the door flew open. Linderman stared at him without expression.

Cliff, his face red and streaked with tears, screamed as he'd never screamed before.

"OKAY! GREAT! YOU WANT YOUR TURN NOW? COME ON, GET IT OVER WITH! I DON'T HAVE ALL DAY! COME ON, YOU BIG, DUMB IDIOT! DO WHAT YOU DO AND GET IT OVER WITH! LET'S HAVE IT, MORON!"

Linderman stared. He stepped aside to let Cliff out. And he stared and stared.

CHAPTER 7

Two hours later, Cliff stood outside Slim's, the coffee shop where most kids from the school hung out.

He could see Willy and Ron at the counter. And he could see Moody and his boys in the back with a lot of other people.

His stomach was shuddering again, but this time it wasn't fear. This time it was excitement, anticipation. He was already enjoying the satisfaction of what he was about to do.

He walked inside and let the door swing shut behind him. He took a deep breath and walked past the counter toward the booths in the back.

"Hi, Cliff," Willy said.

Cliff didn't even look at him. He just kept walking.

"What's the matter with him?" Willy asked.

"Don't know," Ron said. "Maybe he didn't see us."

He stopped when he reached the rear section. Moody's back was to him. Hightower and Dubrow hadn't noticed him yet.

"Hey, Klutz," Moody said, snapping his fingers at a younger kid. "Let's have the fries."

The kid looked at the fries in front of him. "But—they're mine," he said, his voice shaky.

Hightower got up and stood over the kid. "He said he wants your fries," he warned.

The kid handed the plate to Hightower, who delivered them to Moody. He noticed Cliff standing there and grinned.

"Hey, Shelley," Moody yelled, "want to go to the movies tonight?"

"Uh, sure," Shelley said from the next table. "I guess so."

"Hope you have a real nice time," Moody said, covering his potatoes with ketchup.

Everybody laughed, and Shelley blushed. Cliff took another deep breath and propelled himself forward.

"I think we got a visitor," Hightower said.

Moody turned around and looked up. Before he had a chance to react, Cliff had picked up the plate of potatoes.

He pushed the potatoes into Moody's chest and twisted them a few times to make sure they stuck. Stunned, Moody backed away and knocked over his chair.

Cliff picked up a drink from the table and poured it over Dubrow's head. Dubrow screamed, but the laughter all around was too loud for anybody to hear him.

Cliff went for Hightower's burger next. He pounded it with the heel of his hand, sending it squirting out of its roll onto Hightower's pants. As he turned and walked toward the exit, everybody stared at him, amazed.

In three seconds, anger replaced amazement for Moody, Hightower, and Dubrow. Moody led the way toward the exit, Dubrow and Hightower close behind. The rest of the crowd were right behind them.

Moody reached the sidewalk in time to see Cliff turn down an alley. He ran after him.

"I'm going to kill him!" he screamed.

At the opposite end of the alley was a vacant lot. When Moody—and everyone else—reached it, Cliff was standing in the middle of the lot.

Moody, Hightower, and Dubrow ran to the middle of the lot. The crowd followed, but left a little space between themselves and the destruction they had all come out to see.

Moody, his neck and shirt covered with ketchup and pasty french fries, bared his teeth. "You've really bought it this time, Peachpit!" he said.

"Hey, Moody!" The voice came from the sidewalk on the left of the lot. Moody—and everyone else—turned in that direction. All action froze as they watched Linderman make his way to the open space.

He walked slowly, keeping his eyes on Moody. His field jacket flapped in the breeze. His hands hung loosely at his sides, as though he expected to be using them soon. He walked up to Cliff and stopped, still looking straight at Moody.

"Melvin," Cliff said, smiling, "I'd like you to meet my bodyguard.

A murmur from the crowd. Three loose jaws, as the mouths of Moody, Dubrow, and Hightower dropped open. If it were a daydream, Cliff couldn't have planned the reaction better.

"From now on," he announced, "anything you want to say to me, talk to him first. Now, what was it you were saying?"

"Beat it, Moody," Linderman said.

Moody looked at him, then at Cliff. Then he turned to look at the crowd.

The first one to speak was the kid whose fries were decorating Moody's shirt.

"Go ahead, Moody," he yelled. "Show him how tough you are."

"Why don't you invite him to the bathroom?" somebody said.

Moody looked at Dubrow and Hightower. "We can take him," he said.

Dubrow looked at Linderman, then smiled at Moody. "Good luck," he said, and turned and walked away.

"He's all yours, M.M.," Hightower said. He followed Dubrow.

Willy stepped up to Moody. "Moody," he said, "you owe me a year's worth of lunches. You can start paying me back tomorrow."

"Oh, and Melvin," Cliff called. Moody turned to face him. "Your protection services are no longer required. By anyone. Know what I mean?"

"I told you to beat it," Linderman said.

Moody looked around at the crowd. He began backing away. Then he turned and broke into a run.

The crowd cheered. The next thing Cliff knew, people were slapping him on the back and congratulating him. The grin on his face showed his enjoyment. Then he turned and saw Linderman walking off, already a block away.

He broke away from the crowd and ran after him. Even when he reached him, he had to trot to keep up with the long strides.

"Talk about having a fit!" he said, laughing. "Did you see the look on his face when he saw you? Did you love it?"

He gave a little yelp, jumped up in the air, and waved his arms. Then he went back to trotting to keep up with Linderman.

"Thank you, Lord," he cried. "Thank you, Linderman! My father thanks you, my mother

thanks you, my sister thanks you, WE ALL
THANK YOU! Oh, what a great day! Did you
hear what Willy said to him? We're not gonna
let up until he pays back every cent he ever
took from everybody!"

Linderman stopped walking. Cliff was ten
feet ahead of him before he realized it. He
walked back and grinned at Linderman.

"Are you all through now?" Linderman
asked.

"Uh—yeah—what's wrong?"

"We ain't gonna do nothing. Got that?"

"But aren't we—I thought we were sort of a
team now."

"You thought wrong," Linderman said. He
gave Cliff the familiar stony look and walked
away. Cliff stood stock still. He was surprised
and confused. Most of all, he was hurt. He felt
as if he'd just been slapped.

Linderman didn't come to school the next
day. Neither did Moody and his boys, so the
general atmosphere was like that of a party.

In homeroom, Shelley gave Cliff a big smile.
That wasn't a bad beginning for a day. The
back-slapping and congratulating went on all
day long, in classes, in the cafeteria, in the
halls.

It felt good. But not nearly as good as Cliff
might have hoped.

One thing that bothered him was that he
seemed to have been appointed Leader of
something or other. All he'd wanted was to
get Moody off his back. While he was at it,
he'd decided to get him off everybody else's
back too.

What he hadn't bargained for was being

appointed the lifelong opposition to Moody and his gang. He had hoped the problem would disappear once Linderman stood up for him. Now he realized it might not be as simple as that.

Something else bothered him too, and it bothered him a lot more. He still didn't understand what had happened with Linderman after Moody had been taken care of.

When he talked to Linderman about the bodyguard job, he tried to make it clear that the job could be part of a friendship. That's why he offered to do Linderman's homework in return.

But Linderman had only understood the bodyguard part. The friend part seemd to go right by him. That isn't what Cliff had in mind at all.

He went back to his homeroom at the end of the day. Ms. Jump was sitting at her desk, marking papers. He walked in and closed the door.

"Hello, Cliff," she said. "Did you forget something?"

"No," he said. "I wanted to ask you something. Something private, about one of the students."

She put her pencil down and sat back to look at him. "Have you tried asking the student?" she said.

"It's about Linderman," Cliff said.

"Oh. I see. Why do you want to know?"

"Everybody's afraid of him," Cliff said. "And I don't want to be. But there are all these stories, and—"

"There is only one real story," she said. "A couple of years ago, Ricky's little brother killed himself."

"Killed himself?" Cliff gasped.

"It was an accident," she said. "Ricky's father has several guns he uses for hunting. The boy was playing with one of them, and it went off. He shot himself in the head."

It was a few seconds before Cliff could say anything. "How did the stories start?"

"Ricky found the body," she said softly. "I think he was even supposed to be minding the boy, but I'm not sure. In any case, he held himself responsible for what had happened to his brother."

"What about the other things?" Cliff asked. "About killing a cop, and beating up on a teacher, and all?"

"That's all I know, Cliff," she said. "None of that other stuff sounds the least bit believable to me."

The following day, Linderman came in late. Cliff caught up with him in the cafeteria. As usual, Linderman was at a table by himself. Cliff carried his tray to the table, passing Moody and the boys on the way. They didn't look up as he went by.

He put the tray down across from Linderman. "Mind if I join you?" he asked.

Linderman looked off into space and went on chewing. Cliff sat down. He opened his milk and put a straw into the container. Then he took a mouthful of mashed potatoes.

"Yucch!" he said. "What do they call this stuff?"

"I call it garbage," Linderman said, still staring into space.

"Yeah," Cliff laughed. "Uh, Linderman,

would you pass the salt?" No response.

Cliff ate a few more mouthfuls in silence. Linderman still hadn't looked at him.

"Okay," Cliff said. "So maybe we aren't a team. I just got it wrong, that's all. I always thought when a guy does somebody a favor, then the somebody owes him one."

"You don't owe me," Linderman said. He began collecting the remains of his lunch, even though he hadn't finished eating.

"Yes, I do," Cliff said. "I do owe you. You didn't have to do what you did. It's just that I thought that meant we were friends now. I mean, you wouldn't even take money for what you did."

Linderman got up and picked up his tray. Cliff jumped up and put his hand on Linderman's arm.

"Where you going?" Cliff asked.

"Show's over," Linderman said, looking down at his arm. Cliff's hand slid away.

"What show?" Cliff asked.

"You made your impression on Moody over there," Linderman said. "Now the show's over."

He walked out, dumping the contents of his tray at the door. Cliff picked up his own tray and followed him. He caught him at the front entrance.

"Hey, Linderman! That was no show."

"Bug off," Linderman said, taking a cigarette from his shirt pocket.

"Hey, look," Cliff said, "I just wanted to—"

"You just wanted to!" Linderman snapped. The force of his voice made Cliff jump back. "And you always get what you want! I told you to bug off!"

He took a book of matches from his pocket. He opened the door and stepped outside, where he lit the cigarette. Cliff held the door open from inside.

"Hey!" he called.

Linderman tossed the match away and turned to look at him. Cliff nodded toward the burning cigarette.

"Those things will stunt your growth," he said.

Linderman's eyebrows went up a little. Then he turned and walked away.

CHAPTER 8

Roberto eased the Cadillac through the crowded street, while Cliff kept his eye on Linderman. A ball bounced in front of the car. Roberto jammed on the brake, just in time to keep from hitting the little kid who followed the ball from between two parked cars.

The farther they got from the school, the gloomier the surroundings became. They were now passing through a neighborhood that seemed to have a drunk sleeping in every doorway. Small groups of mean-looking guys glared at the limo as it passed by. Roberto was beginning to regret letting Cliff talk him into this.

"If your father knew I was doing this," he said, "I'd be out on my ear. I'll bet even the cops don't walk around here at night."

"Slow down," Cliff said. "You're getting ahead of him."

"We don't want to do that," Roberto sighed. "Why are we following this guy anyway?"

"I told you, I want to find out where he lives."

"Why don't you just ask him?" Roberto said. "What do I know about tailing a guy in the street? It looks a lot easier when they do it on TV."

"Stop!" Cliff said.

Linderman had turned down a narrow street which wasn't much wider than an alley. Roberto slammed on the brake.

"Down there," Cliff said, pointing ahead.

"Are you kidding, Cliff?" Roberto said.
"Look at the size of this thing we're in. There's
no way I'm going to be able to turn it into that
street."

"See you later," Cliff said, jumping out and
slamming the door.

"Cliff!" Roberto yelled. "Cliff, get back here!"

Two men standing in front of a bar began
walking toward the car. Roberto saw them and
shot out for the corner. Maybe he could cut
Cliff off on the next block.

Cliff soon found out there was no next block.
Not the way Linderman was going, anyway.
He followed him into another tiny street, then
through an alley.

He ran past three men sharing a bottle of
cheap wine. The alley led out to a lot, but
Linderman wasn't in sight. He ran to the end
of the buildings, and a hand reached from
behind the corner and grabbed him.

"What are you doing following me?" Linderman barked.

Cliff waited a few seconds until his heart
started beating again. Then he said, "I told
you—I want to be friends."

"I told you I don't."

Cliff decided to talk fast, before he lost him
again. "Look Linderman, I know about what
happened. I mean about your brother and
everything."

There was the almost-smile Cliff had seen
before. "You do, huh?" Linderman said.

"Yeah," Cliff said. "I mean, look, it could
have happened to anybody. It wasn't
your—"

"Drop it!"

Cliff snapped his mouth shut. Then Linderman spoke a lot more softly.

"Just drop it. Okay?"

"Okay. Sorry,"

Linderman took two steps back and looked Cliff over from head to foot. He seemed to be sizing him up for something. Finally, his face broke out into a smile. A real one.

"You want to see something?" he said.

"Sure," Cliff said. "What is it?"

"Come on," Linderman said, heading across the lot.

His strides were shorter than usual. Cliff was relieved that he didn't have to trot to keep up. He looked straight ahead, not saying anything.

They crossed a street, turned a corner, and crossed another street. When they came to a garage behind a gas station, Linderman motioned Cliff to go inside.

A mechanic was working under the hood of a car. When they walked in, he looked up and nodded to Linderman. Linderman nodded back.

He led Cliff to a platform that held some unidentifiable large object, covered with a sheet of canvas. Linderman removed the canvas and stepped back proudly.

It was a motorcycle, but not like any Cliff had ever seen before. It was big and bulky, not as sleek looking as a motorcycle was supposed to be. Then Cliff understood why. It was an old machine, maybe even old enough to be an antique.

"Yours?" Cliff asked.

"Yeah," Linderman said. Even his stony features couldn't hide how proud he was of it. He picked up a rag and polished one of the exhaust pipes.

"Fantastic!" Cliff said. "Do you use it much?"

"Don't use it at all," Linderman said. "It won't run. Go ahead, get on."

Cliff climbed up to the platform. The cycle sat on chocks. Linderman steadied it while Cliff got into the seat. He leaned forward and grasped the handlebars, pretending to be driving it.

'What's wrong with it?" he asked.

Linderman reached over to a shelf and picked out a cylinder. He held it up for Cliff's inspection.

"I can't find the right one," he said. "They don't make them anymore. "I've been putting this thing together for a year, and I'm down to one lousy cylinder."

"You built this?"

"Rebuilt it," Linderman said, putting the cylinder back on the shelf. 'Well, almost, anyway. Come on, we'll do some hunting."

Cliff climbed down and followed him out of the garage. 'Where are we going?" he asked.

'We'll hit a couple of junkyards," Linderman said. "That cylinder's got to turn up someday."

"It'd be great if you could get it working," Cliff said. "You drive up to school on that, you'll knock everybody's eyes out."

"I'm not gonna drive it to school," Linderman said. "I'm gonna use it to get away from here."

'Where you going to go?"

"You name it."

"How about camping in Colorado?"

"Yeah, that sounds good," Linderman said. "Let's try in here."

They were in front of a junkyard. Cliff followed him in, and they walked among piles of metal rubbish. Linderman kept his eyes on the ground, scanning everything as they walked through it. Every once in a while, he'd stop and kick something aside to get a better look at what was under it.

"We went on a fishing trip on Long Island once," Cliff said. "That was when my dad was working in New York."

"Yeah, I'd like that," Linderman said, his eyes inspecting the ground.

"My grandmother says Mexico's real exotic," Cliff said.

"Sure," Linderman said. "That's for me."

"In other words, you'll go anywhere."

Linderman took his eyes off the ground. He looked around past the junkyard, past the block, past Chicago.

"Anywhere away from here," he said.

Ten minutes later, they were in a second junkyard doing the same thing. Linderman stopped to look at the body of an old, beat-up car.

"We had one of these when I was little," he said. "It was old even then."

"What does your dad do?" Cliff asked.

"Watches TV."

Cliff bent down and picked up a cylinder. He held it up for Linderman.

"What about this one?" Linderman shook his head, and they left for yet another junkyard.

"How come you don't talk to anybody?" Cliff asked. "It makes them think all those stories they hear are true."

Linderman smiled at him. "I like it that way. Keeps them from asking dumb questions like you do."

They tried four or five places, with no success. Cliff wouldn't have believed there were that many junkyards in the whole country. Here they were, all in Linderman's neighborhood.

A couple of hours had gone by, and it was beginning to get dark. They came to an auto graveyard, and Linderman stretched out on a pile of useless parts. Cliff sat down next to him.

"My grandmother's the one who raised me," Cliff said, continuing their conversation. "My mother died when I was pretty young. Grandma isn't like anybody you've ever met. She's real old, but she acts like a kid."

"Sort of senile?"

"No, not like that. It's just that she's always playing games, and making jokes, having fun. She causes my father a lot of problems at the hotel. Everybody expects her to act like a little old lady, and she doesn't."

"She sounds great," Linderman said.

"She is. Only my father is worried that he could lose his job. We really have to watch her. She's always into something."

"Well," Linderman said, "maybe she's afraid of being old. Of dying."

They looked through a pile of parts. No luck. Linderman sat on the hood of an old car and looked down at Cliff.

"You want to know about my brother?" he asked.

Cliff nodded. Linderman looked up at the sky then off into space. Then he finally started talking.

"He was only nine. I practically raised him myself. My mother went to work when he was two, and my father—well, he's just my father.

The kid could drive you crazy. Tell him to sit down, he'd stand up. Tell him to do his homework, he'd read a comic book. He couldn't eat food without spitting it all over the place."

He stopped, but Cliff could tell he wasn't finished. After a long pause, he went on.

"He was a good kid. Give you anything he had. He was a real handful, though. Poor little guy."

Linderman was looking at his shoes and shaking his head. Cliff got up and kicked at the rubble. He kicked again, and he saw something that looked familiar.

He bent down and picked up a cylinder. They'd already inspected about 20 just like it, but he held it out to Linderman anyway.

"Any good?"

Linderman looked at it, and his eyes lit up. He grabbed the cylinder and looked more closely. His face broke out into a huge, silly grin.

He hopped off the car and picked up a tail pipe from the ground. Tossing the tail pipe in the air, he let out a whoop of joy.

"Let's go!" he yelled to Cliff. "Let's go put that thing together!"

An hour later, Cliff rode up to the Ambassador East on the back of Linderman's cycle. He had never been happier in his life. He slipped inside without Roberto seeing him.

CHAPTER 9

Linderman carried his lunch tray to an empty table in the cafeteria. He sat down and opened his two containers of milk.

Cliff carried his tray to the table and took the seat next to him. A lot of people watched from nearby tables. They could see Cliff saying something, maybe about the food. Then they saw both of them laugh and dig into their lunch.

Willy picked up his tray from the table he was eating at. He walked over and stood behind Cliff.

"Is it okay if I—."

He stopped, not quite sure what he wanted to ask. Cliff turned and looked up at him.

"Willy!" he said. "Sure. Sit down."

Willy put his tray on the table. He sat next to Cliff. His eyes kept darting from Cliff to Linderman and back.

"What's the deal?" he whispered to Cliff, as though Linderman weren't really there. "We pay him now, or what?"

"No," Cliff said, smiling. "That's all over. Ricky, do you know Willy Carson?"

Linderman—Ricky—looked at Willy, who slid down a few inches in his seat.

"You're the guy that plays the cello," Ricky said. Willy stopped sliding. "I heard you in the auditorium one time. Real nice."

Willy slid back up to his normal sitting height. He grinned.

"Thanks," he said.

When Shelley and another girl joined them at their table, it began to look like any other table in the cafeteria. Most people went back to their own lunches and conversations.

Cliff was having too good a time to notice Moody, Hightower, and Dubrow. They were sitting in the far corner of the room.

If he had seen them, Cliff might have noticed that Moody was collecting money from his two associates. That wouldn't have meant much to Cliff, because he wouldn't have had any idea what the money was for. He never could have known how much trouble Moody was planning for him.

Ricky drove Cliff home after school. This time, they turned the cycle over to a parking attendant and went casually through the front entrance.

Roberto was no longer angry, since Mr. Peache never even realized Cliff was late. Roberto smiled and waved them inside.

Cliff led Ricky to the entrance to the bar. He pointed out his grandmother, who was sitting at the bar, talking to the bartender.

"She'll still be here later," Cliff said. "First, I want to show you my room."

On their way to the elevator, they passed Griffith and an older, very distinguished-looking man. Griffith led the man into the bar and directly to his boss's mother.

"Mrs. Peache," Griffith said, his voice dripping with what he thought was sincere friendliness. "I would like you to meet Mr. Dobbs. He is the head of Hotel Operations."

"How do you do, Mrs. Peache," Dobbs said.

Maybe it was the slight trace of an English accent that did it. In any case, something told the bartender that Griffith was up to no good. He slipped away to call Mr. Peache on the house phone.

"My," Mrs. Peache said, "aren't you a nice-looking fella."

Dobbs was careful not to show any reaction to that. Instead, he said, "Mr. Griffith has been telling me a great deal about you."

"Has he, now?" she said, pleased that Griffith might have paved the way for her with this handsome gentleman.

Griffith took a few tentative steps backwards, like a lowly minister bowing his way out of the royal presence. Mrs. Peache took Dobbs' arm and guided him to the stool next to hers.

"What do you say we have a little drink?" she offered. "Come on! they don't ever charge me anyway."

A smile of complete satisfaction came over Griffith's face. He straightened up, turned around, and glided out of the bar. He went to his office to fill out a purchase order for the new nameplate—the one that would read LESLIE GRIFFITH, MANAGER.

Cliff and Ricky were back in the lobby. They walked past the collection of autographed photos that decorated the entrance to the bar.

"Did you meet all these stars?" Ricky asked.

"Most of them," Cliff said. "I met Steve Martin last month."

"No kidding? Steve Martin?"

"Yeah," Cliff said. "I had my picture taken with him. Come on, there's my father at the registration desk."

As they reached the desk, the clerk handed the house phone to Mr. Peache. Cliff and Ricky got there in time to hear his end of the brief exchange.

"Peache here. My mother! Oh, no! Where? How serious is it?"

He slammed down the phone, leaped over the desk, and ran to the bar. Cliff and Ricky followed.

They ran past the bar and into the lounge. They worked their way around the people dancing to the disco music until they reached a corner with several easy chairs.

Mr. Dobbs was sitting in one of the chairs. His eyes were closed, and he was breathing heavily. His vest and his collar were unbuttoned, his tie was pulled halfway down, and his head rested on the back of the chair.

Griffith was fanning him with a large menu. Grandma stood by, watching.

"Mother!" Mr. Peache said. "What is it?"

"Don't get excited," she said, smiling. "He's all right. He just didn't know his limitations, that's all. I warned him to slow down, but he kept saying he was a dynamo."

Griffith's eyes were on fire as he fanned faster and faster. "Do you know what she's done?" he asked Peache. "Do you know who this is? Your goose is really cooked this time, Peache. She's finally done it!"

He turned to Mr. Dobbs and fanned even faster. "Mr. Dobbs!" he said. "Mr. Dobbs, speak to me!"

Dobbs opened his eyes and caught his breath. He looked up and slapped the fanning menu from Griffith's hand.

"Griffith," he said, "stop hovering over me

like a mother hen!"

"Try to relax, sir," Griffith said. "I'll get a doctor."

"Are you crazy?" Dobbs said, making his way out of the chair. "Get away from me. I'm just getting my second wind." Then, turning to Mrs. Peache, he said, "You can really dance, sweetheart."

The tension drained from Mr. Peache. Cliff and Ricky laughed. Griffith stared at Dobbs.

"You're not so bad yourself, Dobbsie," Mrs. Peache said. "Just a little out of shape is all."

"I know," Dobbs said, straightening his tie and rebuttoning his vest. "That's because I haven't danced for as long as I can remember."

"But Mr. Dobbs—" Griffith said.

Dobbs ignored him. Mr. Peache took Griffith's arm and led him off to the side.

"They're getting along so well, aren't they?" Mr. Peache said. "Why don't you go check on tomorrow's reservations, Griffith? No, wait, I have a better idea. Why don't you go make yourself a reservation? Find yourself a nice, comfortable hotel where you can live while you're looking for a job."

Griffith sputtered, but no words came out. He tugged at his jacket and walked off, trying to project a little dignity as he went. He stepped on the menu, lost his balance, and tripped out the door.

"You just go to your room and get a little rest," Grandma said. "We have a long night ahead of us."

"Oh, all right," Dobbs said. "I'll be back in one hour. You'd better be right here."

"I will be," she said, gently pushing him in

the direction of the elevators. As he left, she turned to the big boy standing next to her grandson.

"You Linderman?" she asked. Ricky nodded. "Care to learn a few new steps?"

"Mother!" Mr. Peache said.

"All right, all right," she said. She stood between the two boys and linked arms with them.

"Come on, you two," she said. "Ice cream sodas all around. I'm buying."

CHAPTER 10

Saturday morning, they met at the park on the lake. Cliff and Willy were there when Ricky drove up. He parked his cycle on the grass and joined them on a bench at their table.

There were dozens of other kids around, most of them from their school. Moody had passed by a little earlier, but Cliff and Willy hardly noticed him. They sat and talked about what to do with the rest of the day.

Moody wasn't far off, in a grassy section that was usually reserved for weightlifters who liked to perform for a crowd. If they had looked in that direction, they'd have seen Moody, Hightower, and Dubrow talking to one of the weightlifters.

They'd have seen Moody reach into his pocket and take out a handful of bills. After he handed the money to the weightlifter, he made his way down to their table.

"Hey," he called, as he approached them, "I've been looking for you guys."

Dubrow and Hightower were right behind him. Following them was a huge mountain of a man. He wore a sleeveless undershirt and tight gym shorts. His head was shaved. His muscles glistened in the bright sunlight.

"What are you looking for us for?" Cliff asked.

"I got somebody I want you to meet," Moody said, grinning. He turned to the hulk. "This is

Mike. *My* bodyguard."

Mike walked over to the table. He ignored Cliff and Willy and held his hand out to Ricky.

"What do you say?" he grumbled.

Ricky stared at his hand. Cliff and Willy stared at Ricky. Ricky looked up at Mike and extended his own hand.

The two huge hands grasped each other and squeezed. Cliff winced. Willy covered his eyes. Ricky and Mike stared into each other's eyes, each determined not to show any signs of pain.

Moody looked from Mike to Ricky, getting more worked up by the second. A crowd of kids had already formed a semicircle around the table.

"Moody here tells me you're a real killer," Mike said. "Beat up on kids and little old lady teachers."

Cliff watched Ricky's face, but there was still no expression.

"Killed his own brother," Moody said. "Got away with it too."

Now the expression changed. But it wasn't what Cliff would have expected. What he wanted to see was anger at the false charge. Instead, Ricky seemed to drift far away from the park. He stared into space, as though he didn't hear what went on after that.

"That's bull!" Cliff said.

"Is that right?" Moody said. "Linderman? Is it bull or isn't it?"

Ricky still looked off at something far away. He had relaxed his grip on Mike's hand.

Mike yanked him forward, pulling him off the bench. Ricky landed on his knees. Cliff jumped from the bench, but Moody stepped over and pushed him back down.

"What are you on your knees for, man?" Mike said loudly. "Begging for forgiveness?" Ricky pulled his hand free. He got up, turned and walked toward his bike. He grabbed the handlebars and began walking it away.

Mike followed him and grabbed the bar behind the seat. Ricky stopped without turning around.

"This is my bike, killer," Mike said. "You got three seconds to get your hands off it."

"Ricky!" Cliff called.

"Shut up, creep!" Moody said.

"One!" Mike said.

Ricky turned his head in Mike's direction. He held on to the handlebars.

"Two!"

The crowd tightened its semicircle.

"Three!"

Mike let go of the bar and punched Ricky in the face. Ricky's grip came loose, and he fell backwards onto the ground. Blood trickled from his nose and his mouth.

Mike stood over him. "Come on, killer!" he said. Ricky stared at the ground. Mike kicked his leg. "Come on, I said!"

Ricky didn't move. Mike walked back to the bike. He yanked off an exhaust pipe.

"No!" Cliff yelled, jumping from the bench. Moody pushed him down, hard enough to make him hit his head on the table. He sat up and rubbed the back of his head.

"You want the bike?" Mike said. "How about taking it in pieces?"

He tossed the exhaust pipe at Ricky. It landed at his feet. Mike pulled off the two directional lights and threw them at him. One of them hit Ricky in the arm. He still didn't move, and he still stared at the ground.

Mike turned to Moody. "I thought you said he was bad!" he yelled.

He put his foot through the spokes of the front wheel. Then he bent down and picked up a large rock. He kicked the bike over on its side. He held the rock over his head and flung it at the bike. It made a deep dent in the frame.

Then he turned to look at Ricky, who still hadn't moved.

"Hey, man," he said, "I'm getting bored with this!"

He picked the bike up and held it over his head. Then he started moving slowly toward the edge of the lake.

"Put it down!" Cliff yelled. He made a move in Mike's direction. Moody grabbed him from behind and threw him to the ground.

Mike tossed the bike into the lake. It landed in the mud, half sunk in water.

Now Moody walked over to Ricky and stood over him. "Look at this guy!" he said to the crowd. "I'm gonna waste him myself!"

He looked down at Ricky, who still hadn't moved. "You want me to waste you?" he yelled. "Yes or no?"

He reached down and grabbed Ricky's hair. He moved his head up and down.

"That looks like yes to me," he said.

With his other hand, he punched Ricky in the face. Ricky fell back onto the ground, blood pouring from his mouth and nose. Mike walked by and looked down at him.

"This is a drag," he said. "Call me if you need me." He went back to work with his weights.

Moody kicked Ricky in the ribs. Ricky groaned and turned over. Moody turned to face the crowd and held up his hands.

"He's a big zero!" he yelled triumphantly.

As he walked away, Hightower and Dubrow ran up and patted him on the back. Cliff went to Ricky.

He knelt and tried to help Ricky get to his feet. Ricky pushed him off. Cliff lost his balance and fell backwards.

They stared at each other for a long time. Then Ricky wiped the blood onto his shirt sleeve and got to his feet. Cliff sat on the grass and watched him until he was out of sight.

The first place he checked was the garage. No, they hadn't seen Ricky all day. He went to a few of the junkyards on his way to Ricky's house. He wasn't surprised not to find him at any of them.

He knew where Ricky lived, but he'd never been to his house before. He found it and walked up the three steps that led to the front door.

The window was open, and he could hear the sound of a TV show drifting out from the living room. He looked in and saw a man sitting in front of the set.

He rang the bell and waited. A woman in a housedress and an apron opened the door.

"Mrs. Linderman?" Cliff asked.

"Yes," she said.

"I'm a friend of Ricky's. From school. I was wondering if you knew where he is right now."

"No, I don't," she said. "He's been out since early this morning. He has his motorcycle with him."

"I know," Cliff said. "Thanks."

"If you find him," his mother said, "will you ask him to call home?"

"Sure, Mrs. Linderman."

He tried the garage again. Then he went back to the park. It was late in the day now, and everyone had left. There was only one reminder of what had happened earlier. The bike sat lodged in the mud.

He walked around a little longer. When it started to get dark, he decided to go home.

Grandma was just leaving for her date with Mr. Dobbs. His father sat in the living room listening to music on the radio. Cliff fell into a chair and stared at his feet.

"Something's wrong," his father said. Cliff nodded. "Want to talk about it?"

After a long pause, Cliff said, "I just don't understand it."

"Understand what?"

Cliff shrugged and looked at his father. "Anything." he said. "Life."

His father smiled. "You're fifteen years old and you don't understand life? What are you, backwards or something?"

"Maybe I am," Cliff said.

"Well, Clifford," his father said, getting up from his chair, "I'll tell you about life. Life is like a great overflowing fountain. A fountain with cool, clear water. But sometimes little birds fly over the fountain. And then the water isn't as clear as it used to be."

They smiled at each other.

"Now you know about life," his father said. "But if you want to talk, or complain, or something, I'm around. Okay?"

"Okay," Cliff said. "Thanks."

He went into his room and sat on the bed. Then he got up and walked out to the terrace. The night was clear, and he looked up at the stars.

A sound behind him made him jump. He turned and saw Ricky standing in the shadows.

"You want to give a guy a heart attack?" he said.

"Cliff," Ricky said, "I need some money."

"Where have you been? I've been looking all over for you."

"Have you got any money?"

Cliff took some bills from his pockets. "Six bucks. It's all I have."

"Thanks," Ricky said, taking the money. "I have to go. You're a good guy, Cliff."

"Wait a minute!" Cliff said. "Where are you going? I'm coming with you."

"No, you're not! You got a nice place, a nice family. Just leave me alone."

"It's the fight, isn't it?" Cliff said.

Ricky's body tensed up. "I couldn't fight. So what? I haven't been in a fight since I was a little kid. I never wanted to be anybody's bodyguard! I told you that!"

"But it's on account of your brother," Cliff said. "It's tied in with that somehow. You can't fight because of what happened to your brother."

Linderman was at the ladder leading to the fire escape. He turned and looked angrily at Cliff.

"What do you know about it?" he hissed.

"What I know is that it's a lousy excuse!"

"Shut up, Cliff!"

"You don't talk to anybody for more than a

year! You walk around like a damned ape—
for no reason at all!"

"Shut up, Cliff,"

"You build a bike to run away to nowhere!
Then you let some jerk just throw it in the
lake!"

"Cliff!"

"All because of something that had nothing
to do with you! Somebody had to find your
brother! So it happened to be you! So what?"

Ricky grabbed him by the shirt. He pulled
Cliff's face right up to his.

"Shut up!" he yelled. "Shut up! I didn't *find*
him! I shot him! It was my fault! I shot him!"

He let go of the shirt, and Cliff toppled backwards into a chair. Ricky leaned back on the
terrace ledge, breathing heavily.

"Oh, no," Cliff whispered.

"I was playing with my father's gun," Ricky
said softly. "I was showing off, teasing him.
He tried to grab it from me. I wouldn't let go.
I was laughing. I was laughing when
it went off! Blood gushed out of the side of his
head. I ran and ran and ran. Then I came back.
I lied. I put the gun in his hand and said I
found him that way."

Ricky's head was sunk into his shoulders.
He looked a foot shorter than usual. He looked
as though he'd just been given another beating.

"I never told anybody before," he said.

Cliff didn't bother to hold back the tears.
They ran down his face. "It wasn't your fault,"
he said. "You didn't mean to do it."

"I let the kid down," Ricky said. "Just like
I let everybody down today. That's the way I
really am."

"No," Cliff sobbed.

Ricky climbed onto the fire escape ladder. Cliff looked up at the stars, trying to imagine what it must have been like to hear that gun go off.

CHAPTER 11

Moody and his boys spent most of Monday spreading the word about Ricky around the school. Moody said only one thing to Cliff all day.

"Tomorrow," he said. "I'm taking care of other business today. But tomorrow is just for you."

After the last period, Cliff and Willy left school and headed for the park. Cliff said he wanted to take one last look at the motorcycle. Shelley caught up with them on the way.

"Where's the funeral?" she asked. "It can't be that bad."

"It's worse," Willy said. "They got my bus fare. They flushed my lunch down the john. They called my mother names I never even heard of before. I'm gonna quit school. I'll never live to graduate anyway."

"Where are you guys going?" Shelley asked.

"To the park," Cliff said.

"I should practice today," Willy said, mostly to himself. "At least they haven't broken my fingers yet. I guess that's next."

As they walked through the zoo, Cliff said, "I just keep thinking there's something I could've done and didn't."

"What more could you have done?" Shelley asked.

"I don't know," he said.

"Look, he'll be back," Shelley said. "He probably just needs some time to think."

"I hope you're right."

"I am," Shelley said, trying to brighten things up a little. "I'm always right. That's something you don't know about me yet. But one day, you'll come to me and you'll say, 'Shelley, you're always right.' "

"Look!" Cliff said, pointing in the distance.

They looked and saw Ricky making his way to the water. He slid down the incline and stepped into the water. He stood in front of the bike and tugged at the handlebars. As they ran up to him, he pulled it out of the mud and onto dry ground.

"I was really scared," Cliff said. "I didn't know what to think."

Ricky stared at the bike. "I couldn't just leave it here," he said.

"You can fix it," Cliff said. "I'll help you."

Ricky brushed some mud off the bike. Cliff helped him get it into a standing position.

Moody, Dubrow, and Hightower walked up to them. Mike stood on a hill, watching.

"No, no, no!" Moody yelled. It was more for the crowd forming behind him than for Ricky. "Leave it where it is! Mickey Mouse doesn't ride a motorcycle!"

Ricky tried to move the bike off, but Moody stood in his way. Ricky tried moving around him. Moody grabbed the handlebars.

He tried to pull the bike from Ricky's grip. They stood staring at each other, both holding firmly to the handlebars.

"Hey, Mike!" Moody yelled. "I can't believe this guy. He just called you a total moron!"

"Moody," Cliff said, "you're real slime."

Mike trotted down the hill. "I was nice to you the other day," he growled at Ricky. "But you're beginning to annoy me."

He pushed Moody out of the way and grabbed the handlebars. He yanked at the bike, but Ricky held fast.

"Some guys never learn," Moody said.

"All right," Cliff said, "enough is enough."

He took a step toward the bike. Moody walked up behind him, grabbed him by the collar, and threw him to the ground.

"You got three seconds," Mike said. "One—"

"Okay," Ricky said.

He let go of the handlebars. Mike grinned. Ricky punched him in the face.

The blow sent Mike staggering back, and he fell to the ground. He wiped his mouth with the back of his hand, then looked at the blood on his fingers.

He stood up and faced Ricky, who had let the bike fall to the ground. They both raised their fists and circled each other.

Mike threw a punch. Ricky dodged it, and Mike's body came sailing toward him. As he flew by, Ricky hit him twice on the side of the head.

With Mike on the ground, Moody made a move toward Ricky. Cliff jumped between them. He and Moody wrestled each other to the ground and rolled along the grass.

Mike got up and stood before Ricky. Ricky threw one more punch, which hit him squarely in the face. Mike collapsed. He fell to the ground and didn't move.

Ricky turned to see Moody pull Cliff to his feet and fling him toward the bike. Cliff fell and rolled down the hill. Ricky bent to help him to his feet.

"Come on!" Cliff said. "I helped you!"

"Oh?" Ricky said, smiling. "Slow down and cover up. Aim carefully and go for his nose."

"But—"

"That's all the help I'm going to give you," Ricky said, shoving Cliff in the direction of Moody.

Both boys bounced around like boxers, their fists raised, and their heads buried into their shoulders.

"Do what I told you!" Ricky yelled.

Cliff moved in closer and waited for an opening. Moody dropped his hands and grinned.

"Come on, Peachpit," he said. "What are you going to do?"

He threw the punch straight from the shoulder. It landed smack on Moody's nose. The blood came so fast that Cliff saw it on his own hand as he withdrew it.

Moody staggered and fell, holding his hands to his face.

"You broke my nose!" he screamed.

Cliff let his hands drop and moved backwards to stand next to Ricky.

"You broke my nose!" Moody repeated.

"I think," Ricky said seriously, "that you broke his nose."

"My nose! It's broken!"

Dubrow and Hightower were standing near Mike, who was just beginning to come to. Moody ran over to them.

"Come on," he screamed. "We can take them."

Mike shook his head, trying to remember where he was. Hightower and Dubrow stared at Moody.

"Come on!" Moody said, grabbing Dubrow's arm. "Let's get 'em!"

"Watch the shirt," Dubrow said, pulling his arm away. "It's new."

He turned and walked away. Moody pushed Hightower in the direction of Cliff and Ricky. Hightower stood fast, then turned and pushed him back.

"Don't ever push me again, Moody," he said. Then he followed Dubrow.

Mike got up, still shaking his head. He began slowly making his way up the hill.

Moody looked around. He started backing away from Ricky and Cliff. The crowd began to break up.

Shelley walked up to the bike. "Let's face it, Melvin," she said. "You just don't have what it takes."

Cliff, Shelley, and Willy followed Ricky out of the park. He moved slowly, pushing the damaged bike ahead of him.

He stopped walking and turned to Cliff. "Can I ask you a question?" he said. "I had this idea."

"What idea?" Cliff asked.

"To pay you to be my bodyguard," Ricky said. "You're some fighter."

Cliff grinned. "Yeah?"

"Yeah," Linderman said. He began pushing the bike again. "I could give you fifty cents a day. And, listen, I could do your homework too. I'm pretty smart, you know."

When they reached the exit, Cliff turned and looked back. Moody was gone. This time, Cliff knew, he was gone for good.